A SCARE IN
THE MARKETPLACE

". . . Suddenly a sturdy Uighur about the same age as Alexi's father, his black and white hat in his hand, was pounding up the aisle toward them. The man waved his hat wildly and grabbed Alexi's shoulder as he jabbered angrily in a strange language.

" 'I'm sorry—I only speak Russian. We just moved to Sukhara,' Alexi explained. . . .

"Then the Uighur jerked Tanya's book bag from her arm. *'Khleb! Khleb!'* ('Bread!') he shouted in Russian, rummaging through the bag. He soon tossed it back to Tanya in disgust and reached toward Alexi's bag.

" 'Tanya, run!' Alexi tore his bag from the man's hand and dashed down the aisle, his sister behind him. . . ."

Other books in this series:
Tanya and the Border Guard
Alexi's Secret Mission

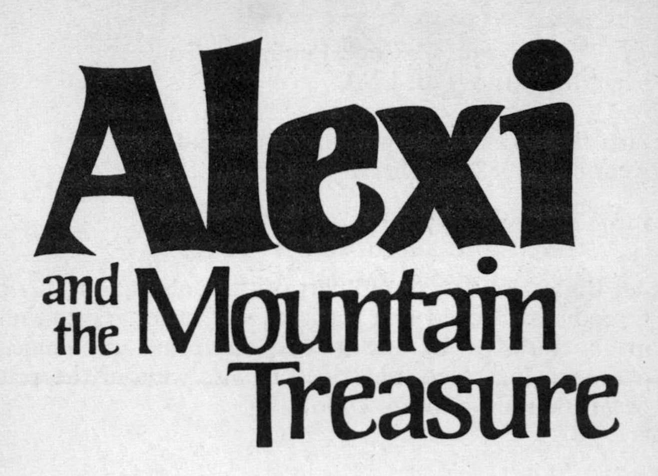

ANITA DEYNEKA

First British Commonwealth edition published 1981
Reprinted 1983, 1984, 1988

ISBN 0 85421 953 6

Printed and bound in Great Britain by
Cox & Wyman Ltd., Reading

To Max Eisenbraun,
who lived and ministered
among the Uighurs.

CONTENTS

WORDS TO KNOW AS YOU READ THIS BOOK

aknan the Uighur word for bread

babushka grandmother, or any elderly woman. Plural is *babushki.*

borsch soup with beets and other vegetables

dedushka grandfather, or any elderly man. Plural is *dedushki.*

Intourist the official Soviet tourist bureau, whose guides are assigned to all foreign visitors

kopeck the smallest Russian coin, like a penny

Uighur (WEE-gur) a non-Russian ethnic group who lives in the Soviet Union and China

religioznik a mocking term for a religious person

ruble the Russian unit of money. One ruble is worth 100 kopecks, or about $1.11.

sibizka a Uighur flute

veruiushchii a Christian believer. Plural is *veruiushchie.*

Young Pioneers the communist youth club for ages 7 to 14

One

THE CHASE IN THE MARKETPLACE

"IT'S OVER HERE, Alexi!" Tanya tugged at her brother's arm, pulling him through the throng of people that crowded Sukhara's outdoor marketplace. She pointed to a stall at the end of the tight dirt aisle. A Uighur man, with a square cloth cap patterned in black and white, stood behind a large pile of flat loaves of bread stacked like pancakes.

"*Aknan! Aknan!* . . . fresh from the oven!" he shouted to shoppers strolling past.

"It's Uighur bread," Tanya said to her brother. "Let's buy some and take it home for supper." She trotted past an apple stand, a stall fragrant with spices, and a shish kebab counter to the booth where the bread was sold.

Alexi pulled his empty book bag from his shoulder and reached inside for twenty kopecks.

"We'll buy that one," Tanya said, pointing to a loaf behind the first stack. The golden-skinned Uighur smiled, balanced the bread proudly in his hands, patted it as if he were saying good-bye, and handed it to Tanya. Carefully, she tucked it into Alexi's floppy school bag.

The children turned from the counter and ambled back through the market toward the street. "Buy! Buy!" A woman in a dress striped like a rainbow smiled and pointed to a pile of watermelons behind her. Then she swiftly cut a dripping sample from one of the melons and handed it to Alexi. Tanya, who had walked ahead, paused by the spice counter and bent to smell the paprika. At the booth beside her, the shopkeeper tied bunches of shining green onions with twigs.

Tanya stood by the vegetable stall waiting for Alexi and watching the shoppers. Close by, an old *babushka* dressed in black bumped down the side of the aisle, clutching a live chicken by its feet. Two Russian boys, their red Young Pioneer scarves tied neatly at their necks, strolled down the path, munching dill pickles. A Uighur girl, several sleek, black braids bouncing down her back, carried a loaf of *aknan*.

Alexi caught up with his sister. "Let's find the

ice cream counter," he suggested, scanning the stalls ahead.

But suddenly a sturdy Uighur about the same age as Alexi's father, his black and white hat in his hand, was pounding up the aisle toward them. The man waved his hat wildly and grabbed Alexi's shoulder as he jabbered angrily in a strange language.

"I'm sorry—I only speak Russian. We just moved to Sukhara," Alexi explained, huddling away from the man's heavy grasp.

Then the Uighur jerked Tanya's book bag from her arm. *"Khleb! Khleb!"* ("Bread!") he shouted in Russian, rummaging through the bag. He soon tossed it back to Tanya in disgust and reached toward Alexi's bag.

"Tanya, hurry! Let's run!" Alexi tore his bag from the man's hand and dashed down the aisle, his sister behind him. The startled Uighur paused a second and then stumbled after the children.

"Try to hide!" Alexi shouted as he darted ahead. He pulled Tanya around a wide, wobbly cart of watermelons that two men were rolling down the dirt path between the stalls.

"Khleb! Aknan!" the Uighur thundered, only steps behind them. But at that moment, a dog dashed in front of the watermelon cart.

"This way!" Alexi grabbed Tanya's arm and swerved her around the cart. The man, too wide to squeeze past the cart, crashed with a thump. Watermelons tumbled on top of him, some of them splitting open. The cart drivers stopped to shake their fists and then scurried to pull their watermelons off the man, who was struggling to stand, his hands and arms waving like a beetle from underneath the pile. The already crowded aisle bulged with people, curious at the commotion.

Swiftly, Alexi glanced back. "We're safe!" he shouted to his sister. "But hurry anyway!" He ran out of the market down the street at a pace that left his sister panting.

They scurried down the cobblestone street so swiftly that people strolling along the sidewalks stopped to stare. They did not stop for several blocks until they had reached the door of their tiny ochre-colored stucco house.

"Alexi! Tanya!" Mrs. Makarovitch exclaimed as she stared at the two flushed, frightened faces. "What happened? Are you hurt?" She bent to feel Tanya's forehead.

"No—it's nothing, momma." Alexi, who was fourteen, suddenly felt chagrined to have been frightened so easily. "We stopped at the marketplace to buy bread for supper. We were walking out of the market, and suddenly . . . it was very strange . . . a Uighur man came running after us. Tanya was scared—and so we ran home."

"Alexi! You were frightened too!" Tanya protested, still trying to catch her breath. "First the man grabbed my book bag, momma. Then he tried to take Alexi's. We ran, and the man bumped into a cart of watermelons, and they fell all over him."

"What did he say?" their mother asked, pushing a strand of hair from her forehead underneath the blue scarf she wore.

"He was shouting something about bread," Alexi answered. "I couldn't understand the rest. He must have been speaking Uighur. It wasn't Russian."

Mrs. Makarovitch turned back slowly to stir the cabbage *borsch* she was preparing for supper. "Alexi, you should have just given the man the bread if he wanted it so much."

"But there were plenty of stacks of bread at the stall, momma. It was strange. He wanted *only* the loaf we had bought."

That night at supper the two told their father about the remarkable experience in the marketplace. "The man with the watermelon cart may still be picking up his spilled fruit!" Mr. Makarovitch said with a smile. "He must wish he could solve the mystery too."

"When the man shouted at us, I was afraid, poppa," Tanya said softly. "He wasn't wearing any special uniform, but he still could have been a policeman of some kind. Remember when the police came to our apartment in Leningrad and took our Bible?"

"Yes, but we're not going to let ourselves be

afraid again," Mrs. Makarovitch said resolutely, speaking as much to herself as to the others. "We're starting a new life in Sukhara. God has led us here."

"Do you remember what Pastor Babitsky told us when we left Siberia to come here?" Mr. Makarovitch asked.

"He said we should be missionaries in our new home," Tanya recalled with an air of pride.

"But, poppa," Alexi said with a frown, "maybe the people in Sukhara don't want to know about God. Most of them aren't even Russian. They're Uighurs. They're so different from us. They're strange! Like that man in the market—I couldn't even understand what he was saying except for the word *khleb*."

"Think of it this way, Alexi," poppa said, pulling his chair closer. "The government won't allow us to travel as missionaries to other countries—to Africa or South America—to tell people about our faith in God. But the Soviet Union is like many countries in one. In the fifteen republics there are 104 different nationalities—people like the Uighurs." Mr. Makarovitch spoke proudly, as if he were giving a speech. It was the same pride Alexi had often heard in his father's voice when he spoke of "our motherland."

"And God loves the Uighurs, too," he added.

Alexi said nothing, but protest surged inside him. He had not wanted to leave Siberia to come to

Sukhara. He did not share his father's hopes about being a missionary to the Uighurs.

By now, his plate was empty, and so Alexi turned to pick up a wooden flute he had started carving months ago in Siberia. With a small piece of sandpaper he carefully smoothed a rough edge.

"Alexi, do you remember the Scripture verse the radio preacher read on the Bible dictation program last night?" Mrs. Makarovitch asked, slipping her arm around her son's shoulder.

Alexi didn't remember. But before he could answer, Tanya had snatched her notebook from its place by the shortwave radio. "I wrote it down," she said, reading the words:

"Go ye therefore, and teach all nations, baptizing them in the name of the Father, and of the Son, and of the Holy Ghost. . . . I am with you alway, even unto the end of the world."

"Are you suggesting that Sukhara is the end of the world, Galya?" Mr. Makarovitch teased, looking over at his wife. "We've only lived here one week."

She smiled, but her voice was sober. "It does seem so far from all the other places we've lived. We're only 175 miles from China."

"And it's only May, and it's already so hot," Tanya complained. "Sukhara is not like Siberia. Are there any lakes we can skate on in winter?"

"I wish we could move back to Leningrad and skate on the canals," Alexi said, remembering the beautiful city where his family had lived before the authorities had exiled them to Siberia. "I haven't seen any canals in Sukhara."

"We must think of it as a geography lesson," his mother said cheerfully. "We have lived in the north and in the east of our huge country. Now we are in the south. We will learn about a new way of life. And you fortunate children will learn a new language. You will study Uighur at school."

"Uighur?" Alexi groaned. "It's impossible, momma." He thought of the Uighur signs placed beside the Russian ones all over the city. He recalled the Uighur newspaper pasted on a billboard that he and Tanya had stopped to study on their way to the market.

"The alphabet is Cyrillic—just like our Russian alphabet," Mrs. Makarovitch said.

"But the words are so different. We'll never be able to read them!" Tanya said.

Mr. Makarovitch was still at the table. "Now, Galya, let's try the famous Uighur bread that was bought with so much adventure at the market today. You may discover, Alexi, that it was worth moving all the way to Sukhara just to eat *aknan*."

Mrs. Makarovitch cut a section from the flat loaf. Her husband broke off a piece to dip in the rest of his tea. But as he did, a piece of paper fell out of the loaf of bread and fluttered to his plate.

Tanya leaped from her chair.

"What's that?"

Suddenly a piece of paper fell out of the bread.

Alexi seized the folded piece of paper and opened it.

"Why would anyone bake a piece of paper inside a loaf of bread?" his mother wondered, peering at the mysterious paper.

"That's why the Uighur man ran after me!" Alexi exclaimed. "He must have known there was a message inside the bread!"

"Read it, Alexi," Tanya commanded, hanging over her brother's shoulder. "What does it say?"

"It's not in Russian. . . ." Alexi puzzled over the paper. "Poppa, can you read this?"

"It's Uighur—like the signs on the stores," he answered as he scrutinized the message. "We need a translator. But we must be careful," he added, a familiar flicker of fear in his eyes. "This message could lead to trouble. We'll have to wait until we find a translator we can trust. For now, we will put it in the drawer and not say a word to anyone."

"But, poppa!" Tanya wailed, staring impatiently at the paper. "How can we wait? The message might be important!"

Two
A UIGHUR FRIEND

"WALK FASTER, TANYA, or we'll be late for school!" Alexi shouted back over his shoulder to his younger sister.

"It's too hot to hurry," Tanya replied as she trudged behind. She swerved each time she passed the wide elms that drooped to the sidewalk so she could walk in their shade.

"In Siberia you always said we had to walk slowly because it was so cold. Now you can't walk fast because it's too hot!" Alexi teased.

But Tanya, wrapped in her own thoughts, seemed not to hear. Alexi understood her sober expression and lagging steps. She was not anxious to reach the new school. For that matter, neither was he.

"I wish we could go back to Narkutsk, back to Siberia," she said softly. "We'll never see the general again . . . or Yuri. And now we have to start another new school, and it is already May and the school year is almost over. We don't know anybody."

But by then the two had reached the school gate, where a huge picture poster of Lenin, the founder of communism in the Soviet Union, was unfurled at the entry. The school itself was a faded yellow. The yard was concrete, but the sun beamed into it, brightening the old building.

In a few minutes the school bell shrilled through the yard, and a rainbow of laughing, chattering students marched into the building. Most of them were Uighurs. Some were Russians. All wore the school uniform—girls in white blouses and dark skirts, and boys in white shirts and black trousers. The Uighur girls plaited their hair in so many long, thin braids that Tanya found she could not count them without staring. Many of the Uighur boys wore square black caps with white designs the shape of almonds embroidered along the top.

Hesitantly, Alexi and Tanya joined the other children filing into the school. Soon they stood at the director's office just inside the door. SONIA ALEKSANDROVNA KURILOVA, DIRECTOR, the sign said. "This must be where we're supposed to enroll," Alexi observed glumly.

"What if she asks if we're *veruiushchie,* Alexi?" Tanya whispered. She tried to remember the brief answer she had rehearsed with her father. She hung fearfully behind her brother, recalling how they had been quizzed only the year before, in Siberia, when they enrolled in a new school.

Sonia Aleksandrovna, a brisk Russian woman with a bun of blonde hair piled on her head, had almost finished filling out the enrollment form when she said, "Are your parents religious?"

Alexi stammered, "Uh . . . yes."

"What religion?"

Alexi scuffed at a paper clip on the floor. "We're Christians," he finally answered.

The director studied the children a moment and then wrote a note on the form.

"Ah, well," she shrugged, "it is unfortunate. I'm sorry to say you will soon discover there are many Uighur students in this school whose parents are also religious people—Muslims. Muhammad or Jesus, they're all the same—dead gods." The director filed the enrollment forms in her desk drawer and stood up.

"But . . . Jesus isn't dead!" Tanya protested, forgetting her shyness for a moment. "We talk to him every day." Alexi squirmed nervously, wishing he could pinch his sister to be quiet.

"Tanya Makarovitch!" the director sternly interrupted. "You will find I try to tolerate religious superstition, but you will not succeed in this school if you talk such nonsense! Now you may go to your classes—but please do not test my patience or your teachers' with such foolish remarks in the future."

A secretary led them in silence down the hall, past a statue of Lenin with an engraving at the base that read, "Lenin is the best friend of children." Inside Alexi's room, the students stood beside their desks waiting for their teacher to enter. They squirmed, wiggled, and talked. But when the teacher entered the door, the rows swiftly stiffened like rows of soldiers until she motioned them to sit. Then she turned to Alexi.

"I'm Tamara Ivanovna," she said with a smile, "and you must be Alexi. You may take the fourth seat in this first row." Like all the other wide wooden desks, Alexi's was shared by another student. His seatmate, a Uighur boy who wore a square cap, smiled. But Alexi looked away and sat stiffly on his side of the bench.

The Uighur boy, Alexi noticed, wore a red scarf—the emblem of the Young Pioneers Communist Youth Organization. In Leningrad and in Narkutsk, Alexi had been the only student in his class who did not belong to the club and wear the red scarf. His communist teachers had been disgusted to have a *veruiushchii* in their classes.

Now, he could not help hoping. Maybe school might be happier in Sukhara—especially if Tanya would keep quiet. He winced at the way she had almost ruined their first day of school in the director's office.

Alexi's teacher now greeted her class by reminiscing about Moscow, where she had gone to university. "At this time of year, the tulips in the Kremlin gardens are beginning to bloom," she said with a sigh. "It is the most marvelous city in the world."

Reluctantly she opened her lesson book. "We will repeat in unison the Young Pioneers membership pledge," she announced mechanically, unrolling a scroll with large red letters. The children with red scarves chanted swiftly:

I, a Young Pioneer, in the presence of my comrades, solemnly promise to love my Soviet motherland passionately, and to live, learn, and struggle as the great Lenin bade us and as the Communist Party teaches us.

The recitation over, the Young Pioneers slid into their seats, and Alexi steeled himself for a lecture from his teacher. There were at least five others, probably Muslims, he thought, who were not wearing red scarves. He wondered if Tamara Ivanovna, like other teachers he had known, would scold those who did not belong to the Young Pioneers.

She did speak sternly—but to a student who was wearing a red scarf. "Igor, how many times have I shown you how to tie your scarf properly? The right side of the scarf *must* be longer than the left." But then, to Alexi's relief, the teacher placed the scroll back on the shelf and said nothing more about the ritual.

Nevertheless, the words of the Young Pioneer pledge, which Alexi had heard many times before, troubled him.

He did love his motherland. Why shouldn't he recite the pledge too? Why was he forced to feel different from the other students?

His father's often repeated explanations broke into his troubled thoughts. "If you join the Young Pioneers, Alexi, you will be required to say that you do not believe in God. How can a follower of Christ deny God?

"Our communist government does not understand. They think we are not loyal to our homeland because we are Christians. It is not true. They do not understand that we Christians have two homelands—heaven and the Soviet Union. We try to be good citizens of both. . . ."

Tamara Ivanovna's voice dragged Alexi's attention back to the classroom. "Today we will continue our study of Uighur history." She pointed to a wide map of the Soviet Union. She motioned to a central southern section of the country and traced with her finger to the Chinese border. "Long ago the Uighur people settled here in Central Asia. Some settled where your city of Sukhara is now located. By the eighth century A.D., the Uighurs had a kingdom of their own. They had their own khan.

"Abdula, what is a khan?" shę asked a boy whose head nodded sleepily.

"A . . . a king," the boy stammered, straightening his slumping shoulders.

"They built walled cities and fought against those who tried to invade them," Tamara Ivanovna continued, her eye on the drowsy boy. "Merchants from Europe and China traveled through the Uighur kingdom. The famous Marco Polo traveled this route from Venice in Europe, and he even learned to speak Uighur. That should be an encouragement to some of you," the teacher said, smiling and glancing, Alexi thought, in his direction.

"In the ninth century, the Uighur people migrated into eastern Sinkiang, into what is now a province of China—just 175 miles from Sukhara," she continued. "There they established a khanate—a kingdom—that existed until the fourteenth century.

"But then the Chinese rulers and the Russian czar took control of the Uighur kingdoms. In czarist Russia the Uighurs were persecuted," the teacher explained, now reading from the textbook before her.

"But in 1917, our leader Lenin and the communists overthrew the Russian czar, and Russia became a communist nation—the Union of Soviet

Socialist Republics. The Uighur people, like all nationality groups in our country, were liberated by the communists.

"There are many Uighurs who still live in the People's Republic of China. Their situation is especially frightful," Tamara Ivanovna said, still reading from her textbook. "These Uighur people are not as fortunate as Uighurs like you and your parents, who live in the Soviet Union, where all people are treated equally. The Uighurs who live in China are not treated fairly by the Chinese government, and most Uighurs there wish they could come to live in the Soviet Union."

As Tamara Ivanovna closed her book, Alexi felt the boy beside him fidget. Then the boy raised his hand, his face burning.

"Yes, Anvar?"

"My grandfather lives in China, and he says it doesn't matter whether we live here or there. He says the Uighurs are still a real kingdom anyway. Grandfather says that someday all Uighurs will be free and live together and rule themselves!"

"Uighur people in the Soviet Union are free *now*, Anvar!" the teacher shot back, glancing over her shoulder as if she feared someone might be listening to the discussion in her classroom. "It is as I have read to you in the book. In the Soviet Union, all 260 million people, whatever their nationality, are equal and free Soviet citizens.

"Now we will discuss another subject," she announced swiftly, before Anvar could speak again.

"For many months we have been studying Uighur history and culture and preparing for our Uighur handcraft contest. You must bring your entries to me by next Friday. The judging will take place at a school assembly the following week. The best entry will be placed in the Sukhara People's Museum, and the creator will receive an important prize," the teacher announced in a tone of awe.

During the day, Alexi snatched glances at the boy beside him. He wished he could ask Anvar for more details about the handcraft contest. But Anvar was a Uighur. Would he even want to talk to a Russian?

Three
A MYSTERIOUS MESSAGE

"MY NAME'S ANVAR," the Uighur boy said with a smile once they were out in the hall at the end of the day.

"I'm Alexi. Have you ever been to see your grandfather in China?" Alexi asked finally after several seconds of silence when he could think of nothing else to say.

"Let's talk in the school yard," Anvar whispered, glancing over his shoulder to see if his teacher was listening.

Outside, Anvar shook his head. "I've seen my *dedushka* once, but not in China."

Before Anvar could continue, Tanya joined the

boys. She had heard the discussion and turned enthusiastically to Anvar.

"We went to Czechoslovakia once to see our grandmother!" she exclaimed.

"I wish I could see my grandfather again," Anvar said. "The last time I saw him I was ten years old. He came with some Kazakh sheepherders across the border. They weren't supposed to cross the Tien Shan Mountains between China and the Soviet Union. But they have secret trails the government doesn't know about, and sometimes the sheepherders come anyway," he explained in a quiet voice. "It's been three years since grandfather came. We haven't had a message from him since. My father is afraid he might have died. But I don't believe it—I'll see him again."

"My mother says she thought we would never see our *babushka* again," Tanya said. "When the authorities gave us permission to go to Prague, grandmother said she believed God had sent us."

"God! Do you believe in God?" Anvar seemed astonished. "Some of my people say they believe in God, but that's just because they're Muslims. Our people have followed that religion for hundreds of years. It's part of our tradition. But most of my friends don't really believe. Even my grandfather doesn't follow the Muslim religion."

"Are your parents Muslims?" Alexi wanted to know.

"No. I wanted to go to the mosque once with some

of my friends, but my father said I couldn't. He's a member of the Communist Party, and he says religious beliefs are old-fashioned and ignorant."

Before the children could continue, a group of Uighur boys walked by and called to Anvar to join them. "Good-bye, Alexi—see you tomorrow!" he called as he hurried toward his friends.

Tanya turned excitedly to her brother when the boys were gone. "We should invite Anvar home, Alexi!"

"Tanya, I just met him today. He's friendly, but we don't know yet if we can trust him. Did you hear what he said? His father is a member of the Communist Party, and he's also a Uighur. We have to be careful!"

The next morning Tanya stood beside her brother's bed. "Alexi! Wake up!" She shook his shoulder urgently. "Listen, I have a plan. Let's invite Anvar home after school today. We don't have any other friends in Sukhara."

Alexi, who always felt grumpy when he woke up, was not excited. "I told you before—we don't know if we can trust him. Besides, what would momma and poppa say?" He rubbed sleep from his eyes.

Tanya was fully awake and enthusiastic. "I thought of that too, Alexi—they always say we can bring our friends home from school."

"Children! Momma says the yogurt and buns are on the table," poppa called from outside Alexi's small bedroom.

"We'll talk about it later," Alexi promised his sister. "But don't say anything until we decide. Momma might worry."

However, that morning the children forgot to discuss their plans as they walked to school. A procession of wooden carts pulled by horses plodded down the street in front of their house toward the market. Uighur farmers from the villages outside Sukhara drove wagons stacked with vegetables, fruit, cotton, and handwoven rugs destined for the downtown open-air market.

Kazakh sheepherders guided other carts loaded with mutton, horsemeat, and a variety of cheeses. One farmer walked beside a stubby donkey with two bundles of fodder tied to his saddle. "The donkey looks like a haystack with legs," Tanya giggled as the animal clopped past, his hooves ringing on the street's spiky black cobblestones.

They watched as people from small stucco houses along the street scurried out to purchase products from the farmers and sheepherders. Soon the street with the burgeoning wagons had itself become a marketplace. Two women with buckets of apples and apricots trudged past the children. "I'm going to dry these on my roof for winter," one of them announced to the other.

By the time Alexi glanced at his watch, he realized that the school bell would ring in eight minutes. "Hurry!" he said, pulling his sister from the excitement of the wagons. "Run, or we'll be late. Give me your book bag so you won't be hot."

Although he sat beside Anvar all day, Alexi couldn't decide whether he should invite him home after school. The two boys had no chance to talk during the classes, which continued with no recess until school was dismissed at one-thirty. During penmanship class, Anvar loaned Alexi some special lined paper. And during Uighur language class, he helped Alexi find the assignment in the bewildering textbook, bulging with strange words.

That afternoon outside the school gate, Alexi and Anvar leaned against the concrete wall.

"Thanks for your help in class today, Anvar," Alexi said. "But I'll never learn Uighur. I'm glad the year is almost over."

"I know how you feel."

"But Uighur must be easy for you."

"We usually speak it at home," Anvar admitted. "But my father has made me study English since I was eight. Now I take special classes two afternoons a week. I can understand many words, but sometimes I think I'll never be able to speak."

As they stood talking, a group of Uighur boys approached. One of them shouted to Anvar in Uighur.

"Not today!" Anvar shouted back in Russian to the boys, who understood that language as readily as Uighur. "I'm walking with Alexi."

Tanya had arrived by then. "Oh, Anvar, does that mean you can come home with us?"

Alexi had decided only a few moments before to follow Tanya's plan of inviting Anvar home. Nevertheless, he glared now at his impetuous sister. Why didn't she find her own friends? Why was she always tagging along and speaking before she thought?

But Alexi went along with her opening. "Yes, why don't you walk home with us, Anvar?" he said, as if that was exactly what he had been planning all along.

"I'd like to." Anvar smiled widely. "Why don't we stop by the marketplace on our way and buy some sunflower seeds?"

Alexi was not eager to return to the marketplace. But neither did he want to explain to Anvar what had happened there. While he was trying to decide what to do, however, Tanya went ahead and told the whole story about the *pani* and the man who wanted it so badly.

"Why did he chase you?" Anvar asked curiously.

"We don't know," Alexi replied. "Let's go on to the market anyway. I'm hungry for some sunflower seeds," he declared, marching down the street.

"The marketplace is beyond your house, and my house is further yet," Anvar said. He stooped to scratch a map in the dirt street when they had given him their address. "We'd better take a bus to the marketplace. Then we can walk back to your house from there."

They squeezed into a blue bus so crowded with passengers that it reminded Tanya of a balloon ready to burst. She edged cautiously away from the door.

They could not reach the ticket box in the middle of the bus. Like other passengers who had climbed on last, they handed fifteen kopecks for their three tickets to a man beside them. "Will you pass this on?" Tanya asked.

The man handed the money to the next person, and it finally reached the ticket box. The woman standing beside the machine deposited the coins, pulled the tickets from the box, and sent them hand-to-hand back to the three students.

"What's the number of your ticket, little daughter?" a *babushka* standing beside Tanya asked. "You know if you get a number seven, you should chew it and swallow it. They say it brings good luck!"

The marketplace was again a kaleidoscope of colors, smells, and sounds. At the sunflower stand, a Uighur sat cross-legged in a stall arrayed with enormous yellow sunflowers, their broad black centers filled with seeds. The children bought one sunflower to share, cracking the shells and eating the tasty seeds.

As they wandered on down the aisle, Tanya's eyes darted from side to side. Was the man who chased them still there . . . lurking behind one of the stalls . . . ready to leap out again?

Later, inside the Makarovitches' cool house, the children heaped their schoolbooks on the table in the room that was used as the living room, dining room, and Tanya's bedroom.

"Momma and poppa are both at work," Tanya explained when she saw Anvar glance around the silent house.

Anvar picked up the wooden flute from the dining room table. "What's this? Does it work?"

"I've been carving it in my spare time," Alexi said. "My father showed me how. It's almost finished. Now I have to find someone to teach me how to play it."

"I know one tune," Anvar replied, lifting the flute to his lips. He played a short, lilting song. "This looks like a *sibizka.* You should enter it in the handcraft contest."

Alexi recalled the teacher's announcement the day before. "Can anybody enter the contest?"

"Everybody is *supposed* to enter. I'm weaving a basket—I couldn't think of anything else. If you enter this, I bet you'll win," Anvar added with a grin, turning to hand the flute to Alexi.

As he did, his elbow scuffed the top of the shortwave radio, which stood close to the table. The red and orange embroidered cloth draped over the radio slid to the floor, exposing a black book underneath.

Anvar hunched over, studying the book. "*Bibliia!*" he exclaimed. "Where did you find it?"

"You've never seen a Bible before?" Alexi asked cautiously.

"Never. But I've heard about them. I know that the Bible is a religious book like the Muslim Koran. But it's impossible to buy one in the stores, and my father says they are very expensive on the black market—like, maybe a month's wages. Can I open it?"

"Of course," Tanya replied. "Go ahead—we read from it every night."

Alexi strode over and closed the shutters at the window of the tiny room. But a large crack gaped between them. "If someone came, they could see us reading the Bible," he worried aloud.

Suddenly Tanya had an idea. "Why don't we go up on the roof, Alexi?" She remembered her surprise when her family had moved here and discovered a ladder leading up to the flat roof.

"It's built that way so people can dry their fruit and vegetables in the sun," Mr. Makarovitch had explained.

Since that time, Tanya had climbed the ladder almost every day. She planned to persuade Alexi to help her arrange the space during the summer into a pretend house or a marketplace. "It would be a perfect place for a fort," Alexi had said when she suggested her idea. "I could go carve my flute there, too."

"There's a ledge around the roof," Alexi said now, weighing his sister's suggestion. "Even if any

"Why do you read the Bible?" Anvar wondered.

of the neighbors are up on their roofs, they wouldn't see us reading the Bible."

Alexi, the Bible in his hands, led the way into the bedroom, up the ladder, and onto the roof.

"Why do you read the Bible every day?" Anvar wondered when they had opened the black book. "My uncle, who goes to the mosque, says the Koran is such a holy book that ordinary people should not touch its cover—only the mullahs, the priests, can open it."

"Poppa says the Bible is like a letter from God," Tanya replied. "Here, you can read it yourself."

Slowly Anvar turned the pages. "Jesus said . . . I am the true bread from heaven. . . ." he read slowly aloud.

"What does that mean?"

Before Alexi or Tanya could answer, they heard a pounding knock on the door downstairs. Swiftly, Alexi closed the Bible and covered it with a basket. "Quiet," he commanded, his finger at his lips.

He recalled the night in Leningrad when Soviet police had come to his family's apartment and seized the Bible a Christian soldier had given them in Czechoslovakia.

Now he glanced again at the basket. His family had been given this Bible by some Siberian Christians who had printed it on a secret press. It had seemed such a good plan to read the Bible on the roof, but if they were discovered . . . Alexi wondered if he could peek over the ledge and see who was at the door. But then the caller might also see him. He sat motionless.

The person pounded again, and a woman's voice called, "Mrs. Makarovitch, are you home? I came to pay back the apples I borrowed yesterday."

"It's the neighbor from down the street," Tanya whispered with a giggle of relief as the woman trudged away from the front door.

Before her footsteps had faded away down the black cobble street, Anvar had pulled the Bible from under the basket and opened it again. For an hour they read and talked. "I wish my parents could read the Bible," Anvar mused. "But they don't read Russian very well. My mother can understand it, and my father can speak it, but that's about all. They read Uighur."

"Maybe there are Bibles in the Uighur language," Alexi suggested.

"Anvar, can you read Uighur?" Tanya asked.

"Of course," Anvar replied. "We always speak it at home. My father taught me Uighur before I was seven, and now we study it at school."

Alexi knew instantly why Tanya had asked. The Uighur note that had fallen from the piece of bread! He hesitated. Should he show the note to Anvar? Poppa had said they must wait until they could find a translator they could trust. But Tanya had already told Anvar most of the story about the man in the marketplace.

"Let's find the note!" Alexi swung himself onto

the ladder and clambered down. "Didn't poppa put it in his bedroom?"

"It's in the top drawer," Tanya answered as she followed him down the ladder.

Swiftly Alexi dug the note from the drawer. "Anvar, remember the story Tanya told you about the marketplace? We didn't tell you what happened after we came home. Momma cut the bread—and there was a note inside. But it was written in Uighur, and we couldn't read it. Here it is."

Anvar's eyes skipped across the page.

"It can't be!" he gasped.

Four
SUMMONS TO THE MOUNTAINS

"ANVAR, WHAT DOES IT SAY?" Tanya begged, her braids bobbing as she stared at the note.

"It . . . it's from my grandfather!"

"Your grandfather! Was that your grandfather who chased Alexi and me at the market?"

"No, no! He must have been a Uighur farmer whom grandfather asked to carry the message to us from across the mountains in China." He paused a moment. "But it sounds like grandfather to think of baking this paper message in a loaf of bread. There would be nothing suspicious about my father receiving a loaf of *aknan*."

Anvar stared at the note, trying to unravel the mystery. "Somehow the messenger must have left the loaf on the counter by mistake or mixed it up with the others, and the shopkeeper sold it to you instead of delivering it to my father."

"But the message itself," Alexi prodded his friend. "What does it say?"

Anvar's voice trembled as he read the Uighur message aloud, translating it into Russian. "Grandfather doesn't know how to write. A friend is writing for him. The friend says grandfather wants to see my father. He has something important to give him—a treasure!

"Grandfather will cross the border with some Kazakh sheepherders when the mountain passes open in early June," Anvar continued, gripping the note. "He will wait in the village of Arba in the mountains for my father to come to see him. Grandfather says he is not well and that *my father must come without fail.*"

"But how can your grandfather cross the border from China?" Tanya wondered. "When we went to Czechoslovakia, poppa showed us soldiers patrolling the border—there were guard towers and fences, and poppa said there were mines with explosives on the strip of land between the two countries. Poppa said all the borders around the Soviet Union are like that."

"It's different on the Chinese border around here," Anvar explained. "The line falls in the Tien Shan Mountains. The mountains are high and rugged. It's impossible to have fences and checkpoints all along the border. There are some marked border crossings, but the Kazakh sheep-herders and Uighur farmers like my grandfather don't use those. They know the authorities would never allow them across, so they find their own paths. They know the mountains far better than the Russian soldiers."

"But is your grandfather well enough to travel?" Tanya asked.

Anvar's black eyes clouded. "I wish father would go see him now . . . in China. He shouldn't wait."

"But it's only two weeks until June," Alexi said.

"Am I ever glad I came to your house and you showed me the note!" Anvar exclaimed. "If you hadn't been my seatmate in school, Alexi, and if I hadn't come home with you, I might never have learned about grandfather coming to Arba."

Carefully Tanya tucked the Bible back under the cloth covering the radio. "Do you think your grandfather would like to read our Bible?" she wondered aloud as she smoothed the cloth carefully over the book.

"Grandfather doesn't know how to read either Uighur or Russian. Anyway, he probably wouldn't listen if I translated to him from a Russian Bible. He says he hates Russians. I remember stories he told me when I was ten. He said the Chinese and Russians conquered the Uighurs and took our land."

"There must be Uighur Bibles somewhere,"

Alexi said. But he wasn't too sure. In the Soviet Union, even Russian Bibles were almost impossible to find. Sometimes foreigners brought Russian Bibles with them as gifts. Once in a while somebody found an old Russian Bible from the years before 1917, when the czar ruled Russia. Now there were the Bibles printed by Christians in Russia on secret presses—like the one Alexi's family had brought with them from Siberia. But these were few and treasured. Alexi had never heard of anyone printing Uighur Bibles.

"I'd better hurry home," Anvar suddenly said, "and deliver this note to my father."

"We'll walk home with you—at least partway—if you want," Alexi volunteered.

Three blocks from the Makarovitch house the students discovered two workmen mounting a wide poster on a billboard along the sidewalk. INTERNATIONAL SOCCER—LENIN STADIUM, the first section of the poster said. The boys read the words eagerly as the men unrolled the rest. TEAMS FROM THREE COUNTRIES BATTLE SOVIET PLAYERS. MAY 30—3 P.M. COME SUPPORT YOUR COMRADES. CHEER THE SOVIET UNION'S GLORIOUS TRIUMPH.

"It's going to be on Saturday afternoon after school. Let's go, Anvar!" Alexi urged. Anvar studied the poster, forgetting his haste to hurry home.

"But the price!" Alexi said as he read the notice at the bottom more carefully. "Two rubles."

"But we could go anyway," Anvar suggested, still staring at the poster. "We'll find a crack in the fence, and we can take turns watching. Besides, the buses will be unloading outside the stadium. Maybe we can meet some of the foreign players."

The next day at school, Alexi knew Anvar's thoughts were in the Tien Shan Mountains with his grandfather and the Kazakh sheepherders. Tamara Ivanovna, more patient than most teachers, had even snapped at Anvar during the Uighur lesson. "Anvar, you seem to have forgotten how to speak your own language. Where are your thoughts wandering today?"

As soon as the final bell had rung and the boys were in the school yard, Alexi asked Anvar the question he had impatiently held inside all day. "What did your father say when you showed him the note?"

For several seconds Anvar did not answer.

"Father won't go," he finally said. "He says he can't, or he will lose his job. He might have to pay a fine or maybe even go to prison. The last time he went to meet my grandfather—three years ago—the authorities found out. They discovered that grandfather had come across the Chinese border without permission, and they said my father was disgracing the Soviet Union by meeting him. China is Russia's enemy. They told father they would be watching him in the future." Anvar faltered, as if he wished he could justify his father.

But then he kicked a stone and sent it skimming across the school yard. "He still ought to go! This might be the last time he ever sees grandfather."

As they walked toward Anvar's house, the children's conversation turned to the happier topic of the soccer game. "We could take the bus after school up to Lenin Stadium. We'll be early, and we can watch the foreign players arrive," Alexi said enthusiastically.

"We can take a picnic along," Tanya added. "I'll ask momma if we can take some of the apples she bought at the market . . . ."

"Soccer is for boys, Tanya!" Alexi protested. "Why don't you stay home and write a letter to Sonia Kovalchuk in Narkutsk?"

"I wrote her last week. Besides, I want to go with you and Anvar."

Her voice was so pleading that Alexi only shook his head and mumbled, "I guess you can come this time."

Saturday was a sparkling, hot, but breezy day—perfect weather for a soccer game. The children had hoped to arrive early at Lenin Stadium, but three buses bursting with soccer fans drove by before one came along empty enough to climb onto. Alexi stared out the window as a Uighur farmer pulled his wooden cart to the side of the road to let the wide bus pass. The sun poured down, but still the man was wrapped in a heavy jacket, and Alexi wondered if Anvar's grandfather might look a little like that bundled old man.

At the soccer field, Russians, Uighurs, Kazakhs, Uzbeks, and others lined up at the gates across from the buses, now parked in symmetrical rows. "How will we know which ones belong to the foreign players?" Tanya wondered.

"I know," Anvar said with a nod. "Follow me. We'll go to the place where the Intourist buses with government guides park. There will be other boys there trying to exchange souvenir pins for chewing gum. Did you bring any pins, Alexi? We might be able to get some gum, too!"

Alexi turned to his sister. "Stay here, Tanya," he said, waving toward a wall near the buses. "You can see everything that's happening, and we'll come find you when we're finished. I'll bring you some gum if we get any."

Surrounded by a swirl of people, Tanya stood forlornly by the wall watching the players troop by in their colorful uniforms. A group of foreign players in blue and white uniforms lined up against the wall. As she watched, she tried to guess where they had come from. America? England? Germany? Did any of them speak Russian?

"Move, little girl! You're in the way!" An Intourist guide shooed Tanya from the wall. "The foreign sportsmen want to take a photo." The guide turned to her companion, another guide, and laughed. "The captain says he wants to send it home to his church. Imagine—an athlete who's a *religioznik.*"

Tanya's thoughts raced. How could she tell who was the captain? Could she talk to him? Would he speak Russian? The players lined in rows in front of the wall. They insisted that one of their members stand alone in the front row.

As soon as the camera clicked, Tanya ran to the man in the front. He pulled a piece of gum from his pocket. Tanya shook her head no. "*Bibliia, Bibliia,*" she repeated. The soccer player looked at her but clearly did not understand.

"Bible? Is that what you mean?" he said finally in English. Tanya took the man's hand and pulled him towards Anvar, who she knew had studied English.

"Anvar—you must try to talk to this man," she panted. "He's a Christian. He speaks English. Ask him if he knows where we can find a Uighur Bible—for your grandfather!"

While the player stood perplexed, Anvar strained to remember his English lessons. "You American?" he asked.

"No, I'm Swedish," the man replied, "but I speak English."

"Ask him about a Bible," Tanya prompted in Russian.

"Do you have a *Bib . . . Bibliia?*" Anvar could not remember the English word for *Bibliia.*

"A Russian Bible?"

"*Uighur* Bible!" Anvar explained.

"Uighur?" The player did not understand.

"Uighur, like me." Anvar pointed to his brown skin and shining black hair.

The player put his hand on the boy's shoulder. "I think I know what you are asking," he answered slowly, so Anvar could understand his words. "But I've never heard of a Bible in that language," he said, opening his hands helplessly and shaking his head from side to side. "Do you understand?"

Anvar nodded his head.

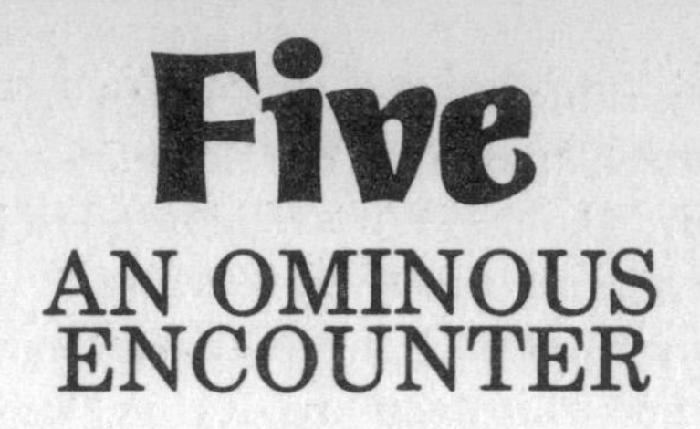

Five

AN OMINOUS ENCOUNTER

MRS. MAKAROVITCH CHECKED TO SEE if the window shutters were locked. Even though the family was still inside the house, she spoke in whispers.

"Yesterday I heard about the brothers and sisters in Rostoff," she said sadly.

"What happened, momma?" Tanya asked.

"The government will not allow them to have a church building. So they sewed a tent together and were meeting in it in the forest. Now the authorities have confiscated the tent. The believers are meeting summer and winter with no shelter.

"But thanks be to God that we have a church here in Sukhara," Mrs. Makarovitch added softly.

She took the breakfast dishes from the table. "Hurry now, or we'll be late for church," she said, pouring the tea remaining from breakfast into a teapot so she could reheat it for lunch.

"Bring your white scarf, Tanya, and I'll tie a bow in your braids."

The church in Sukhara, as Tanya knew from the one time they had already attended, was fifteen bus stops from their house. But at least the Makarovitches didn't have to transfer buses. And after the last stop, they walked only three blocks along a dirt street, where small cottages snuggled together and some Uighur children played near two goats staked in a plot of grass.

The church was behind a high fence. A long, narrow, blue concrete building, it stood in the center of a courtyard.

The singing had already begun and drifted out the windows to the courtyard. Tanya glanced around at the *dedushki* and *babushki* who sat on benches around the walls. "Could we sit in the courtyard during the service?" asked Tanya, pulling her mother toward a bench. "We could hear everything from out here."

"The benches are for the grandmothers and grandfathers," Mrs. Makarovitch reminded as she followed her husband and Alexi inside the church door. The building was filled with worshipers—Russian Christians. But there were no Uighurs, people whom Tanya saw everyday in Sukhara's streets. She wondered if Anvar would be afraid to come with her family to church.

Inside the church, a listless wind fluttered through one of the open windows. A bird had flown in through one of the windows and hovered, chirping, at the back of the long room. Through another window, music blared into the church from a radio turned full volume in the house next door. The preacher had to shout to be heard. The choir sang loudly.

"Why don't those people turn down their radio?" Tanya asked her mother.

"I have heard that the man who lives there is angry that church meetings are held next to his house," Mrs. Makarovitch explained in a whisper. "The authorities encourage him to make noise while the meetings are being held."

Tanya's thoughts strayed from the sermon. Was it the same everywhere for Christians in the Soviet Union? Leningrad . . . Siberia . . . there had always been trouble for her family, just because they were Christians. Poppa had lost his job. They had been exiled to Siberia. She couldn't count the number of times teachers had scolded her and Alexi for not joining the Young Pioneers. She was sure her parents had hoped the struggle would not be so hard in Sukhara.

The meeting was almost finished when one of the preachers asked, "Does anyone have greetings to bring?"

The meeting was almost over when a soldier stood up.

A young soldier in a khaki uniform and stiff collar stood, and people in the front rows turned toward him.

"I bring you greetings from Christians in East Germany, where I am stationed with the Soviet army," the young soldier said. "Now I am home for two weeks visiting my family here in Sukhara. I was not a *veruiushchii* when I left Sukhara. But in East Germany I grew lonely for my own people, my own language. I started to listen to shortwave radio broadcasts and discovered Russian Christian broadcasts from a missionary station in Western Europe in Monte Carlo. It was like God's voice speaking to me from heaven, and I believed."

A rustle of gratitude swept through the congregation.

That afternoon, when the family had returned home, they talked about the young soldier. "Do you think he will be able to find a Bible, Ivan?" Mrs. Makarovitch asked her husband.

"Certainly not here in Sukhara. Perhaps he will be fortunate enough to find one in East Germany. Thank God for the gospel broadcasts. The soldier might never have believed if he had not heard them."

"Poppa," Alexi asked, with a puzzled look, "do you think there are any Christian radio programs in the Uighur language?"

"I don't know. Perhaps the missionaries at the radio stations do not even know that there are such people as Uighurs and so many others in our country who don't speak Russian."

"Why not ask them about it?" Alexi wanted to know.

"Yes--I'll write to Far East Broadcasting Company in the Philippine Islands," his father said. "I'll tell them about the Uighur people and ask them to find someone who speaks Uighur to read God's Word over the radio broadcasts."

"But, Ivan, do you think your letter would reach the Philippines?" his wife asked doubtfully. "What if the censors read it?"

"We will trust God's angels to carry it past the government censors," Mr. Makarovitch said as he moved toward the writing desk.

"I have an important announcement about the Uighur handcraft contest," Tamara Ivanovna said before school was dismissed the next day. Students who had been gathering books and papers, eager for the dismissal bell, paused.

"As you know, tomorrow is the deadline, when all entries must be turned in. But there is a new rule. On the day of the judging, you must be prepared to demonstrate how your handcraft entry is used. For example, if it is a piece of clothing, you can wear it. Whatever you have made, you should prepare a demonstration of its usefulness."

"I guess that means I have to wear my straw

basket," Anvar said with a grin as he dumped his books into his book bag. "You'll win for sure now," he added, thumping Alexi on the shoulder. "Your flute not only looks good, but you can even play it. Tamara Ivanovna will think you're wonderful—and so will the judges."

Alexi shrugged, but secretly, he couldn't suppress a surge of joy. He had finally finished carving his flute and discovered that he did want to win the contest. "But I don't really know how to play the flute yet."

"Don't worry about that," Anvar said. "I know a Uighur song—the one I played at your house. It's easy. I'll teach you. It will be perfect for the contest."

Tanya caught up with the boys. "Anvar, don't you want to win the contest yourself?" she questioned.

"Even if I am a Uighur, I don't like weaving baskets," Anvar replied with a laugh as he gave Tanya's braid a pull.

"Do you like carrying book bags?" Tanya asked. She tugged the bag from her shoulder and held it out to Anvar. "The Uighur textbook is the heaviest. I'm going to be lopsided! I'm glad there are only eight more days of school."

Anvar took the bag, and then he said suddenly, "Why don't you two come to my house tonight for dinner so I can teach you the song on the flute? I'll go home and tell my mother. She won't mind. You ask your parents, and we'll meet at my house. Here, I'll draw you a map."

Alexi and Tanya were both excited to accept his invitation. Later that afternoon as Tanya skipped down the cobble streets toward Anvar's address, she said, "It's the first time we've ever been in a Uighur house. Every time we go by the high walls around Uighur houses I wish I could peek into the courtyard."

"How would you feel if people peeked in the shutters of our house?" Alexi asked, frowning at his sister.

"But we don't have a wall around our house, Alexi!"

"When we first came to Sukhara, I was afraid of the Uighur people—especially after that day in the marketplace," Alexi reminisced. "Then I didn't want to sit with Anvar. But now he's my best friend."

"I think I always liked Uighurs," Tanya said. She bent to pick up a daffodil that had fallen from a wagon on its way to the marketplace.

Anvar's house, like many of the homes in Sukhara, was surrounded by a high cement fence with jagged pieces of glass cemented on the top. "It's to keep thieves away," Anvar explained. The tiny house inside the spacious courtyard was made of mud and straw bricks painted saffron, a color that resembled Sukhara's mountains.

A table stood by a well in the dirt courtyard. A

lanky dog sprawled by the well and lifted an ear as the visitors approached. "His name is Zunin," Anvar said as he scratched his dog affectionately.

Anvar's mother, Mrs. Samedi, a small woman in a bright striped dress of atlas material with a long silk pajama garment underneath, stepped out of the house. She wore dangling, dancing earrings, and her shining black hair hung in a single braid down her back. She walked silently toward the table in embroidered cloth slippers.

She greeted the children in halting Russian but stood shyly back, waiting for Anvar to do the talking. Then she slipped into the house again and returned with several loaves of round flat *aknan,* a pot of green tea, and colorful cups balanced gracefully in her hands. She spoke in Uighur to Anvar.

"My mother says we should eat some bread. She's afraid we will be hungry before father comes home for dinner." He broke off a piece and handed it to Tanya.

Anvar's mother smiled at the three sitting on short stools around the low table. She poured more tea into Tanya's cup but spoke to Anvar in Uighur. Anvar grinned when he translated his mother's words. "Mother says you both look as if you need more sun. She thinks you should sit outside in the courtyard more often."

"I will when school finishes," Tanya promised.

Down the street, high minarets of a Muslim mosque rose to the sky, and a stork perched on one of them. Suddenly he flew from his nest in the minaret toward the Samedis' courtyard. Alexi slowly sipped tea from the bowl Anvar's mother had placed before him and watched the stork. "Sometimes I feel like I've moved to another country," he said. "Sukhara is so different from every place we have lived before. It doesn't seem as if we are still in Russia."

"What do you mean?" Anvar said stiffly. "Sukhara is the land of the Uighurs. That's why *some* Russians feel they don't belong here."

"But I do feel like I belong," Alexi said quickly, reaching for another piece of *aknan*. By now Alexi felt he understood Anvar's patriotism. It was the same sort of feeling that filled his father's voice whenever he spoke of "Mother Russia."

Alexi found his flute and handed it to Anvar. "You promised to teach me a Uighur song."

Anvar played the tune twice through swiftly, his fingers sliding across the tiny holes.

"Do you really think I can learn it in a week?"

"Of course," Anvar said. "It's simple and it's short. It's a tune my grandfather taught me three years ago. I've never forgotten it."

It was almost seven o'clock when they heard a key turn the lock in the gate. Anvar's father, a heavy man in a suit decorated with a row of Communist Party medals, entered. He wore a black and white Uighur cap and stood before the table studying his son's guests.

"So you are Anvar's friends. You are the children who believe in God?" Mr. Samedi said finally, staring at them.

Tanya grabbed her brother's hand.

Six
THE MESSENGER'S STORY

ANVAR'S FATHER IGNORED Tanya's fright. He stared at the children an uncomfortably long time before he spoke again. "I expected that my son would find Muslim friends who were still entangled in religion. But Russians? I thought all Russians were atheists. Didn't your leader Lenin say religion was the opium of the people?"

Alexi couldn't understand this man standing before him. The Communist Party medals on his jacket glinted in the setting sun . . . yet bitterness had tinged his voice when he said, "*Your* leader Lenin." Maybe Mr. Samedi did not trust Russian people. But he worked for the Soviet government

. . . belonged to the party. He was even afraid to disobey the government authorities to visit his own father. Alexi couldn't figure it out.

Anvar's father said no more but, with a shrug and a sigh, sat at the table and waited for his wife to pour him a cup of tea. Anvar spoke seldom to his father, and Alexi sensed a strain between the two of them. He remembered how upset Anvar had been about his father not going into the mountains. Maybe they were still disagreeing about that.

By the time Anvar's mother brought steaming bowls of pilaf—moist rice with meat—carrots, and dried fruit from the cottage, the sun had dropped behind the minarets of the mosque, and the large pot of tea had turned tepid. The courtyard, baked by the sun of the late May day, stayed warm. Nevertheless, Anvar's mother built a small fire in a low stove covered by a grate.

Voices of Uighur families from other courtyards drifted over the stucco walls. Velvet sounds of the *dombra,* a central Asian stringed instrument Alexi had heard nowhere else in Russia, mingled with the conversation. Alexi thought of his flute and wanted to try again the tune Anvar had taught him, but felt too shy to play in front of Mr. Samedi.

Dogs barked in the twilight, begging for scraps of food from families gathered around tables in courtyards all down the block. Zunin settled himself at Anvar's knee when the bowl of fragrant pilaf was set on the table. In turn, everyone reached a hand into the bowl, filling their own dish.

Alexi had eaten three bowls of the spicy pilaf and shared a sliver of carrot with Zunin when he heard the gate into the courtyard creak. Stealthily, swiftly, a man slipped toward the table from the shadows.

"Alexi!" Tanya cried softly when she got a good look at the man's face in the flickering firelight. It was the man who had chased them in the marketplace.

Suddenly it all made sense to Alexi. "There's nothing to be afraid of," he reassured his sister. "He's the messenger. He only chased us because he wanted the note from Anvar's grandfather. Remember?"

The Uighur messenger, dressed in the same white baggy pants, high black boots, and loose shirt tied with a sash, seemed as startled by the sight of the children as they had been by him. Anvar smiled and spoke to the man in Uighur. "I reminded him where he had met you before," Anvar then explained. "He says he remembers the watermelons!"

The man seemed friendly enough, even amused, as he spoke of the incident to Anvar. But he turned suddenly somber when he turned to Mr. Samedi.

"He says grandfather is coming to Arba in ten

days," Anvar translated excitedly in Russian to his friends. "Grandfather is bringing the treasure."

"Hush!" Anvar's father said to his son, with a scowl. "We must not discuss this in front of the Russians."

"But they know already. They met Imur before we did."

Imur, the Uighur messenger, spoke rapidly again, and as he did, Anvar's father grew more distressed. "Father wants to go to grandfather, but he's afraid," Anvar explained quietly to Alexi and Tanya. "Why are grown-ups always so afraid?"

"It's not right!" Mr. Samedi suddenly exclaimed. "A government that separates father and son is not right!" he repeated, his head in his hands.

The Uighur messenger pulled his square hat more firmly to his head and sat by Anvar's father. He spoke again.

"Imur says he is going to tell father a story," Anvar translated. He pulled his stool closer to his guests as the messenger started his tale.

In the days of the Uighur Kingdom, the great Khan Zia was ill. The only medicine that would heal the khan was a magic loaf of aknan. The magic bread was in a mosque in the towering, treacherous Tien Shan Mountains that shadowed the sheepherders. The bread was found in the top of a minaret tower higher than any in the land–so high that now the khan's subjects no longer remembered how it had been built. No mullah or priest went any longer into the minaret to pray.

It was so high that even the bravest warrior quaked at the thought of climbing all the way to the top. And besides, there were huge storks that built their nests in the peak of the minaret. Legend said some were so big they could carry off a man in their beaks. They were enormous enough to scare even a bold man.

The people loved their khan and did not want to see him die. But no man was willing to risk his own life. The khan could have chosen the bravest warriors and commanded them to climb the minaret and bring back the bread, but he was a kindly man and would not do that. He was not like other Uighur khans, who sometimes forced their enemies to climb to the top of minarets and executed them by pushing them from the top.

Each day the khan grew weaker. More doctors and wise men were called to try to save him, but none of their prescriptions helped. The wisest sage, Karamullah, could only repeat, "The cure that will save you is the magic bread from the peak of the minaret."

The khan's family watched sorrowfully at the ruler's bed while the doctors and wise men tried to help. His two daughters wept, but his oldest son, Tursun, a boy of only fourteen, listened to every word the wise man said.

When Karamullah spoke of the magic bread on

the minaret, determination flared in Tursun's heart. He would climb the minaret! He would seize the magic bread from under the wings of the stork and bring it to his father to heal him!

Tursun's mother wept when she learned of her son's plan. "I will lose both my husband and son," she mourned. The khan's bravest warriors accompanied the lad, but no one spoke, and many felt ashamed that they did not have courage like the prince to attempt such a deed.

"It is courage and it is love," Karamullah said simply when he heard of the plan.

"Prince, you must at least wear armor," said the warriors as they tried to persuade the youth, dressed only as he was in his billowing pants, shirt, and sash. "The storks will swoop you away. The stone minaret will cut you."

"And the armor will pull me off the tower," the prince retorted. "Hoist me onto the roof, and from there I will scale the minaret." The warriors obeyed and watched as the lithe young prince clung to the minaret like a spider and slowly crept upward. He moved steadily, his hands hugging the sides, and presently reached the top.

"But still he must face the storks. What will happen then?" one of the old warriors gasped.

A white stork swooped menacingly by the prince and the nest where the magic bread lay. But the prince's billowing black pants and shirt blew like a scarecrow in the wind, and the stork shrieked away in fright. And behold! The prince reached into the nest, seized the magic bread, and quickly climbed down the minaret to the ground, while the warriors cheered wildly.

"So you see," the messenger concluded with a twinkle in his eye, "it is a story about bread, just as our story in the marketplace began. It is also a story about a brave son." He stared steadily at Anvar. "Perhaps it is a sign."

Anvar leaped from his stool. "Father, I *could* go to meet grandfather!"

"No, no, my son! It is not safe for you."

"But the authorities will not be watching me, and summer vacation begins next week. My teachers will never know. It's not so far. It is near the Young Pioneer camp where I went last summer. Please, father . . . please let me go to Arba."

Anvar's mother, in the custom of Uighur women, said nothing when the men spoke, but her eyes betrayed her anxiety.

"But my son, aren't you afraid?" Anvar's father asked, almost gently.

"I am not afraid, father," Anvar answered without hesitating. He placed his Uighur hat on his head.

"Anvar," said Alexi quite suddenly, "I could go with you . . . I would like to."

"And I'll come, too!" Tanya added, standing up from her stool and almost upsetting the low table in her excitement to join him.

Anvar smiled at them both. "Why not? The three of us could go, and maybe even Zunin. Imur will take us in his wagon through the mountains to the village. We could take food and camp along the way."

"But your parents," Mr. Samedi interrupted. "Would they allow you to go? You are Russian children. The ways of the Uighur farmers in the mountain villages are not the ways of a big city like Sukhara."

"I think they will let us go," Alexi responded.

Anvar's mother had understood the conversation. "You are good children," she said, touching Tanya's hand.

When Alexi and Tanya reached their home that night, their parents were not enthusiastic about the trip.

"We must have time to pray about it," Mr. Makarovitch protested. "We can't decide now."

"But poppa, when we lived in Narkutsk, you let Alexi go to a youth meeting in the mountains and deliver Bibles to the church in Tomsk," Tanya said for at least the third time.

"But there was no one else to go."

"It is the same with Anvar. If we don't help him, who will?"

Tanya's mother stroked her braids and pulled her daughter to her. "But Tanechka, even if Alexi were to go, you are so young."

"I'm a year older than I was last year in Narkutsk."

"You are both so young," Mrs. Makarovitch sighed.

Seven
MARCO POLO'S TRAIL

"DON'T FORGET TO TAKE YOUR FLUTE," Mrs. Makarovitch reminded Alexi as he stuffed his books into his school bag the next morning. She held the wooden instrument to the light of the window. "You've worked hard, Alexi, and it's beautiful."

"Anvar says Alexi will win the contest for sure!" Tanya volunteered excitedly.

Carefully Alexi tucked the flute into his book bag. He felt warmed by his family's admiration. Even though he would not have admitted it to anyone—especially to Anvar, who was so casual about the contest—he also felt sure his flute would win the prize. If he did win, the flute would be taken from him and placed in the Sukhara People's

Alexi took his flute to the contest display table.

Museum. But then the other students would envy him. His parents would be proud. And he could always visit the museum and stand by the flute while people stopped to admire it.

Alexi's pleasant speculations seemed confirmed when he reached school and handed the flute to his teacher. "This is superb. Did you carve it all by yourself?" she asked, tracing the design etched in the wood.

"Yes," Alexi said quietly.

"Can you play it?"

"I'm going to play a Uighur tune the day of the contest. But until then, I still have to practice every day after school."

He walked to the contest display table and placed his flute beside two teacups painted with triangular purple and yellow designs. He studied the other entries and compared them to his flute—several embroidered Uighur hats, beads, pottery, baskets, shawls, clay sculptures. He was so engrossed in his comparisons that he did not notice Anvar standing beside him.

"What did your parents say? Can you come with me to Arba?"

"They didn't say yes, but they didn't say no, either" was all Alexi had time to whisper before the first bell rang.

"We won't discuss it again until poppa comes

home," Mrs. Makarovitch said when she returned from work that afternoon, a string bag full of market vegetables in her hands. Both Alexi and Tanya were standing at the door waiting to talk about the trip to the mountains.

"I bought some *aknan* at the market this afternoon," she said, changing the subject. "I was almost afraid to buy it when I remembered all the adventure that started from one loaf of bread!"

When Mr. Makarovitch arrived home, he too was reluctant. "Let's not discuss it until after we have read the Bible and listened to the gospel broadcast," he said. "Perhaps something from God's Word will help us decide."

At supper Tanya gulped her bowl of *borsch* and hoped her haste would help her father open the Bible sooner. But he was hungry and happy. "It's good to be back to engineering again," he reflected. "It's not that the collective farm in Siberia was all bad, but I'm trained to be an engineer. . . .

"I'll have some more *borsch*, Galya," he said, holding up his bowl. He broke off a piece of *aknan*. "Russian *borsch* and Uighur bread. What could be a better combination?"

When Mr. Makarovitch finally reached for the Bible, he opened it to the Book of Psalms.

"O God, in mercy bless us. Send us around the world with the news of your saving power and your eternal plan for all mankind. . . ."

"You see, poppa!" Tanya exclaimed. " 'Around

the world'—that's just like going into the mountains by China."

"It *is* like going around the world," her mother agreed.

"I think you're eager to interpret the Scriptures in favor of your trip, Tanechka," her father said, closing the Bible. "But now it is time for the broadcast. We must postpone our discussion until later."

Alexi bent to turn the knobs. "There's jamming tonight, poppa," he said, frowning at the dials.

But through the static noises, they could hear the faint words of the speaker drift in and out like waves on a shore. ". . . Jesus replied: 'I am the bread of life; no one coming to me will ever be hungry again. . . .' "

"Bread, poppa." Tanya nudged her father. "It's a sign!"

"Tanya, shh!" her mother scolded. "You know you shouldn't talk during the broadcast."

But as soon as Tanya's father had switched off the radio, her thoughts flew swiftly. "Don't you see, poppa? It's just like the story Imur the messenger told last night about magic bread. It *must* be a sign."

"It will be their summer vacation time soon," Mr. Makarovitch mused, turning to his wife. "They won't miss school. Surely children are permitted a holiday in the mountains. All the Young Pioneer children go to camps in the mountains. Our children should be safe with the messenger.

He must be a good man if he has taken so much trouble to bring Anvar's father the message."

"And Imur said he would hide us in the wagon until we were out of the city. We're going on a road he calls Marco Polo's trail!" Tanya added merrily.

"But you must take along clothes warm enough for the mountains," Mrs. Makarovitch said. "A Uighur man at the market told me the mountains cool quickly at night."

"Momma! We can go?!"

"Not before the second day of vacation. Alexi must play his Uighur song in the handcraft contest. And I need some time to prepare."

"And there are many questions to be solved before then," Mr. Makarovitch added. "I should meet Anvar's father and the messenger, Imur. How far into the mountains is the village of Arba? And what's this about Imur hiding you until you are out of the city?"

Eight

ALEXI'S FAMOUS FLUTE

"ALEXI! WAKE UP! It's the day of the contest," Tanya shouted, jerking her sleeping brother from his bed. "How can you sleep? I'm so excited! I hope the whole school comes to the contest."

"Tonight I am bringing home a box of Russian chocolates—the best in the world," Mr. Makarovitch announced when the family sat in a circle around the breakfast table. "Whatever happens at school, we will have a little celebration. This family has already decided the winner."

Inside the auditorium where the contest was to be held, Alexi's teacher stood at the door directing students to chairs. When she saw Alexi, she tapped him on a shoulder and smiled. "Sit in the first row, Alexi. You should be ready to go to the front if your name is called."

When the auditorium was full, a man with medals and ribbons shining on his jacket walked onto the stage. The rows of students quieted. "This is our judge—Comrade Neskov from the Central Committee of the Sukhara Communist Party," Alexi's teacher announced grandly, directing the judge toward a chair.

Alexi, his heart beating hard, waited and tried to concentrate on the other students as they demonstrated their entries. A Uighur girl, Zelena, modeled a striped skirt made of atlas material. Several wore Uighur hats they had embroidered with colorful threads. Anvar trudged across the platform carrying his basket.

When his name was called, Alexi tried swiftly to rehearse the Uighur tune in his mind. He was certain he had memorized it completely. If only he could recall it calmly now. He walked to the front, stood at the center of the platform, and lifted his flute to his lips.

A loud squeak shot miserably through the auditorium. Alexi's hands shook as he lowered the flute.

"Go ahead, Alexi," Tamara Ivanovna said quietly from the chair where she sat behind him.

Alexi's hands still shook, but he began again and played the tune flawlessly this time. Since it was short, he repeated it twice.

As he finished, he heard Comrade Neskov exclaim, "That flute looks like a real *sibizka!*" Then the ringing, reassuring sound of clapping reached his ears and followed him to his chair. From a back row, Tanya even waved, but Alexi tried not to notice.

Ten more participants paraded across the platform, and then Tamara Ivanovna and the judge conferred for several minutes.

"And now the winners," she said finally. Anvar nudged Alexi.

"I won't win," he whispered. "I made that mistake on the first note."

"Third prize to Zona for her handpainted teacups!" There was loud applause as Zona marched to the front to claim her certificate.

"Second prize to Ulio for his embroidered hat!" Tensely Alexi watched the boy come forward from several rows back.

Then—"And first prize goes to my newest student—Alexi Makarovitch for his wooden flute!"

The students stomped and cheered as Alexi strode in a cloud of happiness to the platform.

"You are to be commended, Alexi Makarovitch," the Communist Party official said. "It is a great honor for your flute to be placed in the Sukhara People's Museum. . . . However, little comrade," the man's voice assumed a slightly darker tone, "I do have one observation I must make, or I would be negligent. I am sure it is just carelessness on your part. But still I am surprised. On such an important occasion as this—where is your red scarf?"

The official's words hung in the air of the crowded auditorium. Alexi felt fear and anger creeping through him and knew his face was crimson. Tamara Ivanovna looked down at the platform and said nothing. The man stared at Alexi and waited for an answer.

"Well, did you forget your scarf at home, young comrade?" he finally prodded.

"No," Alexi said sullenly.

"Where *is* your red scarf?"

"I don't belong to the Young Pioneers."

"Don't belong!" The crowd of students sat silent and stunned as Comrade Neskov turned abruptly to Alexi's teacher. "We can't award the first prize to a boy who doesn't belong to the Young Pioneers. It would be a poor example."

A fire flaming inside him, Alexi clutched his flute and stumbled to his chair. From a distance he heard Ulio, the boy with the embroidered cap, summoned to the front to receive the first prize.

When the assembly was finished, Alexi could not move. He sat staring at the floor.

"I'm sorry, Alexi," Anvar whispered. "It wasn't fair. But it's just a silly contest anyway. Who cares? In a few days we'll be on our way to Arba. Just try to forget it."

Alexi held the flute in his hand as if it were a

serpent. "I'll forget it . . . I'll forget everything," he said savagely, flinging the flute into a nearby wastebasket.

Through the crowd, Tanya pushed toward her brother. "Alexi! Alexi, don't!" she cried when she saw him hurl his flute. But Alexi had already fled out the door. While the others around her stared, Tanya searched in the basket until she found the flute.

Nine
A FRIGHTENING EXPERIENCE

"SUKHARA MAY BE NEAR THE DESERT, but even the desert freezes in wintertime," Mrs. Makarovitch fussed as she folded two woolen sweaters into the small satchel that the children planned to carry on their trip.

"But momma, it's summertime now," Tanya reminded.

"It doesn't matter. You will certainly need warm clothes at night in the mountains!" She wrapped five loaves of *aknan* in sheets of newsprint and placed them in the satchel on top of the clothes.

Alexi picked up his flute and tucked it in the

satchel. He hadn't touched it since yesterday—since the handcraft judging. But as soon as he had flung the flute away, he had been sorry. He was secretly relieved that Tanya had retrieved it unbroken.

The thought of the contest still stabbed him, and he had not felt like talking about it—even to his own family.

But, in his own way, he had thanked Tanya. "If you want, I could teach you how to play Anvar's Uighur song this summer," he had offered.

Early the next morning the two told their mother good-bye and began their walk with the satchel to the marketplace. Horse-drawn wagons and carts from the mountains laden with mounds of fruit and vegetables had already started to arrive, bumping slowly down the cobblestone streets. "What if Imur's wagon is loaded down like that?" Tanya worried. "There won't be any room for us."

"There's Anvar!" Alexi said, waving. They hurried toward their friend, who stood by a sauerkraut stand. Women with empty jars waited in a line for the shopkeeper, who ladled out spoonfuls of salty cabbage.

But suddenly Tanya spied another familiar figure walking toward them in the aisle. "It's your teacher—Tamara Ivanovna!" she gasped, grabbing Alexi's arm.

"Good morning, Alexi," the woman said. "And is this your sister?"

"Yes, this is Tanya," Alexi replied politely, restraining his first impulse to run.

"And how are you two spending your summer vacation?"

"We're helping our parents and traveling to visit friends," Alexi replied calmly.

"I too am traveling. In two days I will return home to Moscow and stay until school begins. I wish you a happy summer," she said with a wave as she walked away.

Anvar, who had darted behind a sunflower seed stall when he saw his teacher, waited until she was safely out of sight before he approached Tanya and Alexi.

"Of all days to meet Tamara Ivanovna!" he groaned. "Now we must be careful she doesn't see us meeting Imur."

"She's so excited about going home to Moscow. I'm not sure she would even notice," Alexi said.

"Let's stand in the shade," Anvar suggested, leading Tanya and Alexi from the insistent sun that shone steadily on the eastern corner of the market.

"Imur said to wait here," Anvar whispered as they came to a fruit stand, where a *babushka* sat cross-legged in front of the stall, snoozing in the sun. "Fresh cherries for sale," she cackled, awakening as the children approached. Rhythmically she swatted flies with a twig.

Three short, sharp whistles rang through the

air. Anvar turned swiftly to see Imur beckoning with his hand to a cart. "Let's go. He's ready," Anvar said, trotting toward the wagon. With relief, Alexi saw that his teacher was nowhere in sight. He climbed quickly into the wagon and held out a hand to help Tanya over its sideboard and onto the wagon floor, where homespun Uighur rugs were stacked in high piles with a space in the center.

"Imur says we should sit here between the stacks of rugs until we're out of the city," Anvar instructed. "Then no one will notice us and stop to ask questions. Otherwise, someone might wonder what you two Russians are doing in a Uighur wagon."

"For this trip we'll pretend we're Uighurs," Tanya replied with a laugh.

Imur stepped onto the hardboard seat at the front of the wagon and shook the reins of his two horses, who stood in the hot sun flicking flies with their tails.

As Imur steered the horses through the narrow market street and out into the city, Alexi peeked around a stack of rugs. A yellow and blue Volga followed slowly behind the wagon. "It's a police car!" he gasped. He struggled to think calmly and to silence the fears he felt clawing inside.

The police could not know why he and Tanya and Anvar were going into the mountains, he tried to convince himself. Or did they know? What if they questioned Anvar? Had they discovered Anvar's grandfather crossing the border through the mountains from China without permission? Maybe they had already caught Anvar's grandfather—and found the treasure he was bringing.

"The car's still there! Quick! Let's pull some carpets over us," Anvar ordered. Alexi felt terror throb through him as he lay still, forcing himself not to look from under the carpet. For his family, encounters with the police had almost always brought danger and heartache.

Within minutes the policeman had pulled up beside the wagon. "Hey, farmer!" he bellowed at Imur. "Pull over to the side of the road."

"Oh, Alexi! It's so hot I'll suffocate," Tanya whispered from under her rug. "I'm scared!"

"Don't move! Don't say a word!" was all Alexi had time to whisper before the policeman had stepped out of his car and was marching toward Imur.

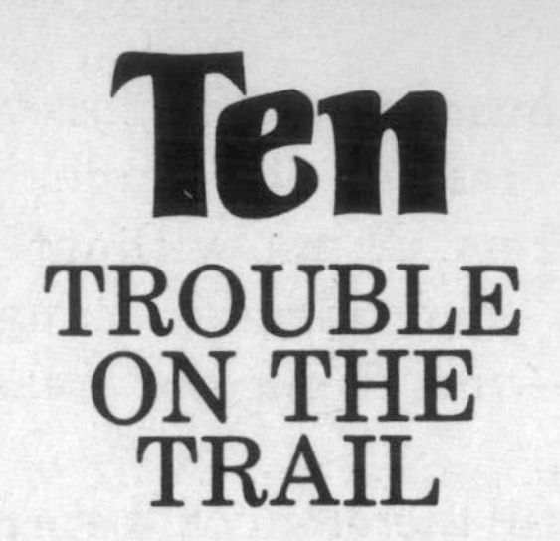

Ten
TROUBLE ON THE TRAIL

"WHERE ARE YOU GOING, FARMER?" the policeman wanted to know.

Imur, who understood a little Russian, pointed toward the mountains. "Home," he told the officer.

"Show me your passport," the policeman demanded, showing Imur his own passport from his pocket as an explanation. "You know you must carry your passport at all times—and especially whenever you travel like this." He took one quick, curious walk around the wagon.

Imur fumbled with the buttons of his thick jacket.

"If you don't have it, you know I'll have to search your wagon," the policeman added.

"He's telling us to stay hidden," Anvar hissed.

Why is it taking Imur so long to find his passport? Alexi worried silently as he stretched in his hot hiding place under the rugs. *What if he forgot it?*

"Oh, so you sewed it into your jacket! All right, old farmer. Drive on to your village. You have a long trip through the mountains."

Imur clicked his tongue, and the horses moved ahead. Immediately he started to sing.

"He's telling us in the song to stay hidden under the carpets," Anvar hissed. "He says when he stops singing, it will be safe for us to come out."

The police car stayed close behind the wagon for two miles more while the children sweated. It was only when Imur had finally weaved the cart through the city traffic onto the mountain road that the police car drove past, and Imur stopped singing.

"Come out!" Imur called finally to Anvar. "We're safe now—on Marco Polo's road!"

Alexi glanced swiftly around the carpets to the road behind the cart. "No cars in sight," he said, wiping sweat from his face.

Tanya fanned her face with her hand. "Isn't Imur hot? Why does he always wear that heavy jacket? He must be roasting!"

"Uighur farmers say their jackets keep them warm in winter and cool in summer," Anvar explained, propping his feet on a pile of the colorful rugs. "Grandfather told me that once."

As the wagon wobbled up the road, the children

stretched out on the wagon floor. They talked, ate *aknan,* and watched other wagons from Uighur villages coming down with fruits and vegetables for the market in Sukhara. A few times Imur nearly collided with another wagon on the narrow road.

At one place, they spotted some fruit that had fallen from the heaped cart of a Uighur farmer ahead of them. Imur stopped his cart, jumped from the wagon seat, and collected the fruit and vegetables. "It isn't the horse, it's the oats that pull the wagon," he chuckled, storing the free food in a box on his cart.

"Alexi, why don't you play your flute?" Tanya suggested timidly after a while. "Maybe Imur knows the words to Anvar's song."

As the wagon clattered up the mountain road, Alexi played the haunting melody several times. Imur swayed and whistled on the wagon seat but only shook his head when Anvar asked if he knew the words.

"The song sounds so sad. But I'll make up happy words," Tanya said playfully. "It will be a game. Everybody has to write one verse of a song." She sat in a corner humming to herself. Finally she sang:

This is Marco Polo's route.
Marco played his flute.
He sang and played and tapped his boot
All the way to Droot.

"Droot? What country is that?" Anvar asked.

"Oh, it's somewhere beyond the Tien Shan Mountains," Tanya answered loftily. "Besides, it rhymes with *flute*. Now it's *your* turn, Alexi!" But he and Anvar only stretched out in the wagon and laughed at her song.

As the dirt road wound deeper into the forest, the mountains loomed larger. During the day, the sun crept in and out of the clouds until evening, when it slid swiftly behind a distant mountain.

At sundown, Imur pulled his wagon to the side of the road by a stream that gurgled from the mountain. "We're going to camp here—in the Valley of Laughing Water," he announced. Soon he was gathering twigs to build a fire, and singing as he worked.

"It's a Uighur song," Anvar explained when he noticed Tanya trying to understand Imur's words. "The song says,

Fine, fine children!
Just give me time
You'll have supper,
And even a whistle.

Imur scooped a kettle of water from the stream and suspended it on a stick holder above the fire. From a box he pulled a small square brick of green tea, pressed together and pungent. He cut a slice and dropped it into the boiling water. Then he wrapped some potatoes in leaves and put them in the campfire.

It took almost two hours for the potatoes to bake, but when they had cooked, they were flaky and delicious. Imur and the children sat content and cross-legged around the campfire just as they would at a Uighur table—sipping green tea, eating potatoes and *aknan*. "To hurry is not polite," Imur chuckled, savoring each sip of his tea.

Off in the dusky distance, the soaring snowclad Tien Shan Mountains shadowed the sky. Alexi gazed at the mountains. Usually he enjoyed the sight of them. But that night they rose foreboding before him as he thought of Anvar's grandfather coming from China, struggling to cross the twisting border through the mountains secretly and reach the village of Arba.

Was it worth the risk? What treasure was the grandfather bringing? Jewels? Money? A secret message?

"In geography class, my teacher said that the Tien Shan Mountains are twenty-three thousand feet high," Tanya said, disrupting Alexi's thoughts. She too thought about the grandfather who at that moment was probably somewhere on the mountain trails.

"Grandfather's Kazakh friends who are guiding him across the border know the trails like mountain goats," Anvar said, as if he were trying to reassure himself.

"Has Imur ever crossed the Tien Shan Mountains?" Alexi wondered, flipping a stick into the campfire.

"Many, many times," Imur replied after Anvar had translated the question. "The name *Tien Shan* means 'Mountains of Heaven.' But they are also treacherous mountains, with steep ravines, floods, mud slides, falling trees, wild animals, and even bandits.

"I remember once coming through the mountains at night with a load of valuable carpets. I turned a bend in the road, and suddenly four bandits with guns jumped onto my wagon. . . . But I shouldn't tell you my experiences. It will just frighten you."

"Bandits!" Tanya suddenly was wide awake. "Are there ever bandits on *this* road?"

"Sometimes."

"How much longer before we reach the village where your grandfather is coming to meet us?" Tanya asked anxiously, scooting closer to the campfire.

Imur took a deep drink of tea before he answered. "We have now passed the Russian villages and houses. Soon we will be among Uighur people. Tomorrow we will drive all day through these low mountains. We will pass through some settlements of Kazakh sheepherders."

"Are they your people too?"

"We're all related," Anvar explained. "We are

all Turkic people. The Kazakhs live in the mountains. They're sheepherders and nomads. The Uighurs live on the lowlands and are farmers. After we pass through the mountain settlements of the Kazakhs, we will still travel one more day to the bottom of the mountains . . . until we come to Arba."

Imur unrolled four carpets around the campfire. "We'll start as soon as the sun rises tomorrow."

Then he gestured toward the wagon and spoke to Alexi. Anvar again translated. "Imur asks if you will play your flute while he falls asleep."

Alexi rose from his crouched position beside the campfire and walked toward the back corner of the wagon, where he had placed the flute that afternoon. He reached behind the carpets near a box of food but could not find it. He felt under the carpets and along the wooden floor.

"Anvar! Bring a flashlight and come help me search."

The light followed his fingers along the wooden floor as he traced a wider circle from the corner. "I'm sure I put the flute in this corner," he said. "Oh, no! Look at this!"

He wedged his hand through a large crack in the floor. "My flute must have jolted over the crack and fallen through. And I didn't see this crack because it was covered with a rug."

For another half hour, Tanya held the flashlight on the wagon while the two boys and Imur, who had by now joined the search, looked under every rug and box on the wagon.

"It's no use. It's fallen through the crack somewhere along the road." Alexi kicked the wooden wagon wheel and trudged back toward the campfire. He wondered now how he could have ever considered throwing the flute away.

Without music, Imur and the children slowly settled to sleep on their soft carpets around the campfire. No one spoke of the lost flute, but Alexi discovered he could think of nothing else as the last embers faded and he finally fell asleep.

It was noon the next day when Imur guided the wagon around an abrupt bend in the mountain road. His two horses almost stumbled into a band of sheep stretched across the road and out into a meadow. Kazakh sheepherders, who wore black hats that dangled with several strings like sheep tails, followed the animals.

In the distance, Kazakh tents, or *urtas,* made of wood saplings covered with black felt material, dotted the meadow. On a slope by the side of the road, three Kazakh women in long colorful skirts and shawls pounded a bag of wool to make felt covering for the *urtas*. The smell of cooking mutton drifted from the tents.

Imur reined his two horses to the side of the road and spoke with the sheepherders.

"How can they understand each other?" Tanya asked.

"It's a Turkic language like Uighur—they're all similar," Anvar answered, listening to the conversation.

The Kazakh sheepherders pointed to Alexi and then to Tanya. Imur replied rapidly, gesturing to them.

"They are asking if you are Young Pioneers who have come to help herd sheep," Anvar explained. "Sometimes they come from the camps for a few days as a work project. Otherwise, the sheepherders meet Russians only when they take their meat and cheese to sell in the city."

As Imur and the sheepherders talked, a wagon piled with clothes, buckets, soap, pots, leather, and other products from Sukhara stores pulled up behind them. Alexi watched as the men started to unload their wagons and carry their purchases to their *urtas*.

"Alexi!" Tanya cried so loudly that Imur stopped speaking in the middle of a sentence. She pointed wildly to one of the sheepherders who was unloading the wagon. "It's your flute!" she cried, leaping toward the startled man and grabbing for the instrument.

The sheepherder seized the flute, his black string hat shaking. He spoke angrily to Imur.

"He says he found the flute on the road and it's his," Anvar translated.

"But—it's mine!"

The man shook his head furiously and spoke

louder, as if that would help Alexi understand the Kazakh language.

"He says he found the flute and it belongs to him now. It's the custom of the mountains. He says he is going to take it the next time he goes to the marketplace in Sukhara and sell it."

"Sell it! But it belongs to Alexi!" Tanya protested.

Imur gestured, talked, and bargained with the man while the children stood listening, straining to understand.

"The sheepherder has agreed to sell it to us," Anvar said after the men had talked a long time. "For five rubles," he added slowly.

While Anvar spoke, the sheepherder stood stolidly by his wagon, grasping the flute and looking pleased to have a possession someone wanted so much.

"Five rubles!" Alexi dug furiously in his pocket, knowing he would find nothing more than the fifty kopecks—half a ruble—his father had given him for the trip.

Alexi held out the money to the sheepherder. Maybe he would feel sorry and change his mind after all. But the sheepherder glanced disdainfully at the kopecks. Accustomed to bargaining at the marketplace, he firmly held up five fingers, as if Alexi did not understand the price, and clutched the flute more tightly.

Stubbornly, Alexi held up three fingers. "Do you

think Imur would lend me 2½ rubles?" he whispered to Anvar.

"I don't think he has any. He just has carpets to trade. And the sheepherders already have plenty of those."

Alexi dug his foot into the dirt. "Anvar, I have an idea!" he exclaimed after several seconds of silence. "Remember the gum we traded from the foreign soccer players at Lenin Stadium? Do you have any left? Tanya, where are the pieces I gave you?"

"I've got three left," Anvar said reluctantly, but he handed the gum to his friend.

"And I've got five." Alexi counted them under his hand so the sheepherders would not know the extent of his treasure. "With Tanya's, that makes ten altogether."

Like an experienced trader, Alexi added six sticks of gum to his fifty kopecks and held out his offer to the shepherd.

"More!" the man demanded, pointing to the gum.

Alexi added his last four pieces of gum and eagerly held out his hand for the flute.

With a satisfied smile, the sheepherder reached for the gum and returned Alexi's flute.

"This time, I'm holding it all the way to Arba and back," Alexi yelled, leaping onto the wagon.

But Imur and the children had traveled only a few miles from the Kazakh camp when they heard hooves pounding the road behind them.

In seconds, a horse and rider thundered into sight. "It's the sheepherder," Alexi cried, stiffening. Swiftly he hid his flute behind his back.

"He's chasing us—he's coming closer!" Tanya screamed. Imur's stories of bandits told around the campfire swept through her memory.

Eleven
THE TREASURE REVEALED

TANYA SHOUTED TO IMUR. "Faster! Go faster!" But it was too late.

The sheepherder reined his horse to a halt and leaped onto the wagon beside Imur. He waved his hands and shouted while Tanya cringed in a corner of the wagon.

Abruptly, he turned from Imur and held out his hand to Alexi. Alexi stepped back swiftly, hiding the flute behind him.

The sheepherder scowled and muttered to Imur, who started to laugh—so heartily that Tanya thought he might tumble from the driver's seat.

Anvar, who had been trying to decide what was

happening, finally understood the sheepherder's words. "He wants to shake your hand, Alexi." Anvar laughed too. "It's the Kazakh custom. The sheepherder says he never makes a bargain without sealing it with a handshake."

Hesitantly, Alexi held out his hand.

The sheepherder shook it solemnly, jumped on his horse, and was gone as swiftly as he had come.

During that day, Imur and his three passengers passed several more Kazakh settlements. It was not until the next morning that the road wound out of the mountain into a valley. Anvar sat on the driver's seat beside Imur and leaned forward.

"Do you think grandfather got to Arba safely? What if he hasn't come yet? What if something happened and he couldn't come? What do you think the treasure is?" Alexi could not remember his friend ever having been so talkative.

It was early afternoon before Imur finally announced, "Do you see those red roofs in the distance? That's Arba!"

Fields of wheat, maize, oats, and vegetables stretched out from a cluster of white stucco houses with bright roofs. The settlement nestled at the bottom of a low range of mountains dwarfed by the gigantic Tien Shan border mountains behind.

"The Soviet government calls Arba a collective farm," Anvar observed scornfully. "But my people owned this land long before the Russians. I wonder where grandfather is staying."

Imur knew the street and house. He urged the tired horses to the place where he had been told Anvar's grandfather would wait. The door into the stucco house was low, and Imur stooped as he followed after Anvar, who had flung himself from the wagon and into the door without stopping to remove his shoes.

Alexi, his satchel in his hand, followed timidly behind. Now that they stood at the doorstep, Tanya felt fearful. "Maybe Anvar's grandfather won't like us, Alexi. Remember what he said. His grandfather doesn't trust Russians."

A short Uighur *dedushka* with a crusty face the color of the lowland mountains and eyebrows as hairy as his head stood in the room. He embraced Anvar and kissed him three times. He nodded absentmindedly when Anvar introduced Alexi and Tanya but looked beyond them as if he were expecting someone else. Anvar shook his head and sadly explained why his father had not come.

His grandfather studied them all for several seconds. Then he spoke, accenting the soft syllables of his Uighur language with sharp gestures. He motioned Alexi and Tanya out toward the door.

"He wants us to leave," Tanya whispered.

"I'm sorry . . ." Anvar started to say, but he could only glance apologetically at his friends before his grandfather beckoned him to sit on a rug on the floor.

Outside in the courtyard, Alexi and Tanya settled themselves on a low bench under a willow tree. They could still hear the grandfather asking questions and urging long replies from Anvar, all in Uighur.

"I wonder what they're talking about," Tanya said forlornly. The trip through the mountains had been an adventure, but here in the Uighur village, face to face with Anvar's stern grandfather, she felt lonely.

Alexi, however, was looking for something to fill the time. "I think I'll play my flute," he said, reaching inside the satchel he had carried from the cart. The melancholy Uighur tune was the only tune he knew, so he played it again and again.

"Alexi, why don't you learn another tune?" his sister said irritably, wishing he would stop playing his flute and talk. "I'm tired of that song. I've heard it so many times."

Alexi began the song again. But before he had finished, Anvar's grandfather appeared in the doorway. He listened intently. Then the old man hobbled toward them.

He pointed to the flute and spoke rapidly to Anvar, who had followed him from the house. "Grandfather wants to know where you learned that song," Anvar translated. "I told him I taught you."

The grandfather settled himself beside Alexi. "Play the song again," he commanded.

As Alexi played, the grandfather started to sing

in Uighur. His voice cracked and wavered, but he knew every word. "Again!" he demanded and sang another verse as everyone listened to the haunting melody.

"The words . . . they're strange," Anvar said slowly when his grandfather had finished singing. "I'll ask grandfather to repeat them, and I will try to translate for you."

Beyond the highest mountains,
Fierce with shining snow,
Is there a heavenly trail
Where a man after death can go?

Down to the deepest valley,
If I struggle, search, and climb,
Is there a heavenly treasure
For a man from earth to find?

At last I will walk
To the mountain's heavenly crest,
But what man knows the way
To a homeland after death?

"Those words are mine," the grandfather said slowly when Anvar had finished translating. "I wrote them ten years ago when your grandmother died. Again and again I sang the words when I was alone herding sheep in the mountains. I had forgotten that I taught you the melody, Anvar."

For several seconds no one spoke. Finally, the grandfather stood. A trace of a smile touched his face. He spoke to Alexi and Tanya. "Grandfather invites you to come into the house with us," Anvar said. "He wants to give you bread and salt. It's a symbol of friendship."

Alexi fell in step with Anvar as they followed the grandfather toward the house. The solemn words of the grandfather's song stayed in Alexi's thoughts, troubling him in ways he had not expected. He thought of the hopeless expression in the old man's eyes as he had sung. He remembered hearing his own father say, "It is the same, Alexi, for every person—Russian, Uighur, or any nationality. Every person was created by God. No person can be happy until he finds God and ends his search."

The Uighur house had no curtains at the windows and no furniture. The main room was sunny and also barren except for bright woven rugs decorating the floors and walls. Imur and the young people sat cross-legged on the floor while the grandfather walked into another room. He returned carefully holding a small, square, wooden box in his hands.

"Anvar, did you read the message I baked in the *aknan* and sent to your father?"

"Yes, grandfather. Alexi and Tanya read it too."

"I told you I was bringing a treasure to Arba—my greatest wealth." He sat on the carpet, placed the box in the center of the circle, and opened it reverently. He lifted a packet from it wrapped in white silk. Then he pulled several thin yellow sheets of paper from the wrapping and held them in his hand.

"Now I will tell you the story of these pages. Forty years ago, a foreigner came to Uighur lands from far away. He told me about a God, a father of all peoples. He gave me these pages. He said they would guide me to the God who lives in the land after death.

"Now I am an old man, and soon I will die. But I cannot read these. I know how to read no language. And I had no one I could trust to read them for me.

"So, Anvar, I am giving them to you and your father. More than anything, I want to find the God who lives in the land after death. But I am afraid it is too late for me. Now I am giving my greatest treasure to you," he repeated, handing the pages ceremoniously to the boy.

Anvar held the pages gently so they would not crumble. "Grandfather, this is written in Uighur! It's an old alphabet, but I can still read it," he said, straining over the pages.

Anvar read slowly, "Jesus said, 'My father gives you the true bread from heaven.'

"Those words—" Anvar stammered, translating them into Russian, "aren't they from the Bible?"

Alexi could only nod his head yes.

"Grandfather! Grandfather!" Anvar cried. "The

Bible God *does* speak Uighur!" He swiftly told the story of Alexi and Tanya's Bible and how he had read it on their rooftop.

Gently, the old man took back the yellowed pages and held them in his hands. "Your friend will play my song once more on his flute," he said finally to Anvar, who swiftly translated the command to Alexi.

While Alexi played, the grandfather slowly repeated his song:

Beyond the highest mountains,
Fierce with shining snow,
Is there a heavenly trail
Where a man after death can go?

Down to the deepest valley,
If I struggle, search, and climb,
Is there a heavenly treasure
For a man from earth to find?

At last I will walk
To the mountain's heavenly crest,
But what man knows the way
To a homeland after death?

When he had finished singing, he still cradled the crumbling pages of Uighur Scripture in his hands. Then he spoke, staring out the door at the Tien Shan Mountains, distant and dark.

"All my days I have lived in the shadow of the Tien Shan. Many lives before mine, our ancestors, searched to find the heavenly secret of the Tien Shan.

"The Uighurs searched. The foreigners invaded. They took our rugs, our spices, our furs, our jewels—our treasures," the grandfather said in a chanting voice. "But one foreigner *brought* me a treasure.

"I did not know. The secret of the Heavenly Mountains lay hidden . . . buried in my little box . . . locked in the Bible book . . . .

"Then, Anvar, you and your Russian friends came," the grandfather continued as if he were a bard reciting a ballad. "Now I will know the secret . . . you and your father will know . . . someday all our people will hear.

"Now, you will read the words of the Bible God," the old man commanded. Carefully he passed the pages to Anvar. "Now you will open the treasure to me."

EPILOGUE

ANVAR'S PEOPLE, the Uighurs, live in the Soviet Union and China. There are an estimated six million of them, mostly on the plains of the Sinkiang Uighur Autonomous Region of China near the borders of Russia. About two hundred thousand Uighurs, however, live on the Soviet side of the border, many in the city of Alma-Ata in Kazakhstan, U.S.S.R.

The Uighurs, a Turkic people, have lived for centuries in Central Asia, in the cradle of land surrounded now by the U.S.S.R., Mongolia, and the People's Republic of China. This remote and fabled region has been a crossroads of Eurasian civilization.

Before recorded history, nomads roamed this rugged terrain. Later Genghis Khan and Tamerlane, the Mongol conquerors, invaded. The famous Marco Polo explored and held Westerners spellbound with tales of Central Asia's treasures and wonders. The Silk Road, the exotic caravan route of medieval times that Marco Polo traveled, wound through Central Asia, linking this landlocked area to the outside world.

Central Asia is still in many ways a mysterious, inaccessible area. Little is heard in the Western world about the Uighurs and other nationalities who live there, such as the Kazakhs, Kirghizians, and Uzbeks.

The Uighurs who live in the Soviet Union are only one of 104 different ethnic groups in that vast country. These diverse peoples speak a wide variety of languages. In fact, in the late 1960s the Soviet Academy of Science published a five-volume report listing 127 languages spoken within the U.S.S.R., the world's largest country.

Although the Russian language is taught and used throughout the Soviet Union, many of the non-Russian ethnic peoples prefer their own language and resist studying the official Russian language. Consequently, it is estimated that almost a quarter of the U.S.S.R.'s total population neither speak nor understand the Russian language very well.

Over the last 100 years, churches, missions, and

Bible societies have printed Bible portions in 40 of the 127 languages. But that still leaves almost 50 million Soviet citizens, many of them Muslims, without any Scripture. This is an enormous and compelling spiritual need.

Christians in the West can help supply Scriptures and gospel radio programs for Uighurs and others in the Soviet Union. Translation has now begun on the New Testament in Uighur and other minority languages.

If you are interested and wish further information, write:

Slavic Gospel Association
27 Vicarage Road
Eastbourne
East Sussex
BN20 8AS